Victor's *Adventure*
in Alphabet Town

by Janet McDonnell
illustrated by Pam Peltier

created by Wing Park Publishers

CHILDRENS PRESS®
CHICAGO

Library of Congress Cataloging-in-Publication Data

McDonnell, Janet, 1962-
    Victor's adventure in Alphabet Town / by Janet McDonnell ;
illustrated by Pam Peltier.
      p.   cm. — (Read around Alphabet Town)
    Summary: Uses many words beginning with the letter v to
describe the caring relationship between Victor the Vet and his
animal patients.
    ISBN 0-516-05422-8
    [1. Veterinarians—Fiction. 2. Animals—Fiction. 3.
Alphabet.] I. Peltier, Pam, ill. II. Title.
PZ7.M1547Vi 1992
[E]—dc 20
                                  92-4036
                                    CIP
                                    AC

Victor's *Adventure*

in Alphabet Town

You are now entering Alphabet Town,
With houses from "A" to "Z."
I'm going on a "V" adventure today,
So come along with me.

This is the "V" house of Alphabet
Town. Victor the Vet lives here.
He is an animal doctor.

Victor loves "v" things. His house
is filled with them.

Victor likes to play the

violin.

And he likes to send

valentines.

But most of all, Victor likes being
a vet. Every day, he hops in his

van

and goes to visit sick animals.

Victor the Vet makes them better.

Victor always keeps treats in his pocket. He gives one to each animal he visits.

And he always plays his violin to cheer up the animals. Everyone loves Victor the Vet.

One day Victor visited a bird. She had lost her voice. She could not sing.

Victor gave the bird some vitamins.
"Give her two a day," he said. "Her
voice will come back soon."

Then Victor visited a giraffe. The giraffe had a sore throat. Victor gave her some medicine.

He also gave her some vanilla ice cream. "It will feel very good," he said.

Next Victor visited a cat. Her tail was stuck in a

vacuum.

Victor took out her tail.

It did not hurt at all. "Be very
careful around the vacuum," said
Victor.

When Victor was all done visiting
the animals, he hopped in his van
and went home.

The next day, Victor the Vet did
not visit any animals. His van did
not move. Victor was sick.

When the animals found out, they came to visit Victor.

The bird gave Victor a

v-neck sweater.

The giraffe gave Victor a velveteen pillow.

The cat brought Victor
his favorite

videos.

Then the animals gave Victor a giant card. It said, "For a very special vet. Get well soon."

"Thank you all very much," said
Victor. "I feel better already."

Victor felt so good, he began to
play his violin. The giraffe and
the cat danced to the music.

And, thanks to Victor's vitamins,
the bird sang along.

MORE FUN WITH VICTOR

What's in a Name?

In my "v" adventure, you read many "v" words. My name begins with "V." Many of my friends' names begin with "V" too. Here are a few.

Valerie

Vern

Vivian

Van

Vicky

Vinnie

Do you know other names that start with "V"?
Does your name start with "V"?

Victor's Word Hunt

I like to hunt for "v" words. Can you help me find the words on this page that begin with "v"? How many are there? Can you read the words?

vine

veil

olive

train

raven

doll

villain

Can you find any words with "v" in the middle?
Can you find two words with no "v"?

Victor's Favorite Things

"V" is my favorite letter. I love "v" things. Can you guess why? You can find some of my favorite "v" things in my house on page 7. How many "v" things can you find there? Can you think of more "v" things?

Now you make up a "v" adventure.